Eject Eject Eject

First published in 2010
by Evans Brothers Limited
2A Portman Mansions
Chiltern Street
London W1U 6NR
UK

Printed in China

British Library Cataloguing in Publication Data
Phillips, Dee, 1967-
        Eject, eject, eject. -- (Right now!)
        1. Fighter pilots--Afghanistan--Fiction. 2. Fighter plane
        combat--Fiction. 3. Young adult fiction.
        I. Title II. Series
        823.9'2-dc22
        ISBN-13: 9780237541965

Developed & Created by Ruby Tuesday Books Ltd

Project Director – Ruth Owen
Head of Design – Emma Randall
Designer – Emma Randall
Editor – Frances Ridley
Consultants – Lorraine Petersen, Chief Executive of NASEN,
and Antony Loveless
© Ruby Tuesday Books Limited 2010

ACKNOWLEDGEMENTS

With thanks to Lorraine Petersen, Chief Executive of NASEN
for her help in the development and creation of these books.

Images courtesy of Shutterstock; **pages front cover, 1, 3, 10-11, 13 top,
14, 15 bottom, 18-19, 20, 21, 37, 40-41, 42-43** Antony Loveless.

While every effort has been made to secure permission to use copyright material, the publishers
apologise for any errors or omissions in the above list and would be grateful for notification of
any corrections to be included in subsequent editions.

Suddenly, we saw a missile.
It was heading straight for us.
A heat-seeking missile!
We were under attack.

Eject Eject Eject

I'm as cold as ice.
It's so dark in this cave.
Dark and icy cold.
A storm roars outside.
The wind howls.

Icy water drips from the
roof of the cave.

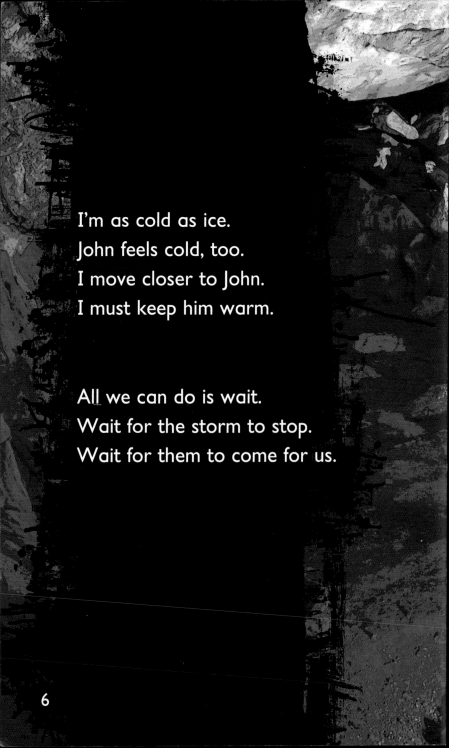

I'm as cold as ice.
John feels cold, too.
I move closer to John.
I must keep him warm.

All we can do is wait.
Wait for the storm to stop.
Wait for them to come for us.

John moans in pain.
His legs are broken.

I say, "We'll be OK, Mate."

I say, "We'll soon be back
at base. I'll buy you a beer
when we get there."

All we can do is wait...

We were on a mission.
I was in the pilot's seat.
John was the navigator.

WE WERE FLYING LOW.

LOW AND FAST.

Suddenly, we saw a missile.
It was heading straight for us.
A heat-seeking missile!
We were under attack.

I broke left.

I broke right.

I tried to shake off the missile.
But it was still heading
straight for us.

15

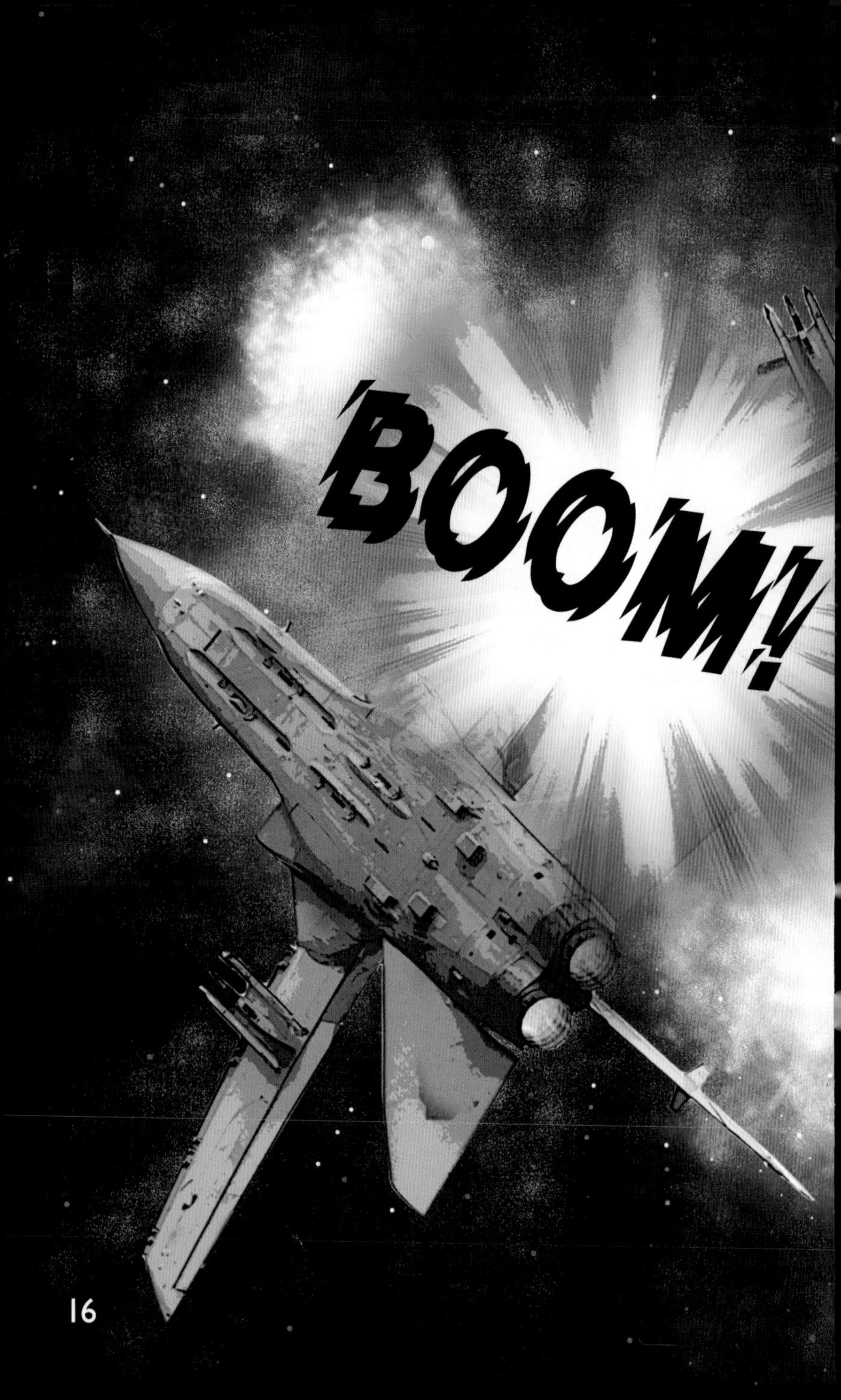
BOOM!

The missile hit us.
We lost our left wing

We were spinning.

We were falling.

We were burning up.

Spinning

Falling

Burning

We had to get out.

I shouted,

"Eject

Eject

Eject."

I pulled the eject lever.
Straps pulled tight on my arms and legs.

BOOM!
The plane's
canopy blew off.

BANG!
I shot out
of the plane.

I flew into the air
like a rocket.

I'm as cold as ice.
It's so dark in this cave.
Dark and icy cold.
John feels very cold.
I must keep him warm.
He's in a lot of pain.

I say, "We'll be OK, Mate."

Icy water drips from the
roof of the cave.

I am so cold.
So cold and tired.
I want to sleep.
But I must stay awake
for John.

All we can do is wait.
They will come soon.
They will come when
the storm stops.

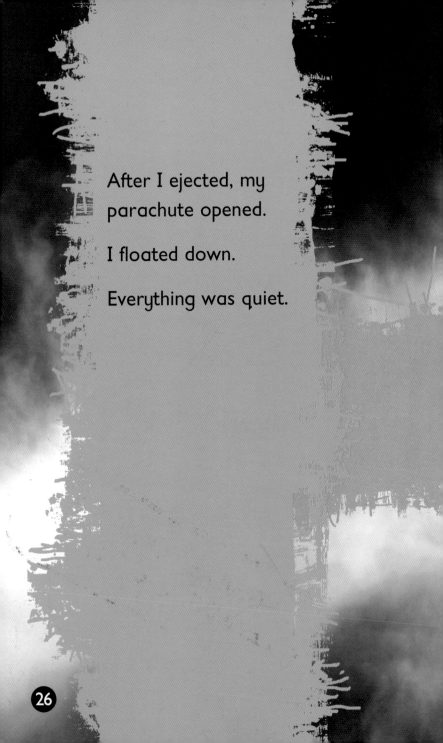

After I ejected, my
parachute opened.

I floated down.

Everything was quiet.

But where were the enemy fighters?

Where was John?

I hit the ground hard!

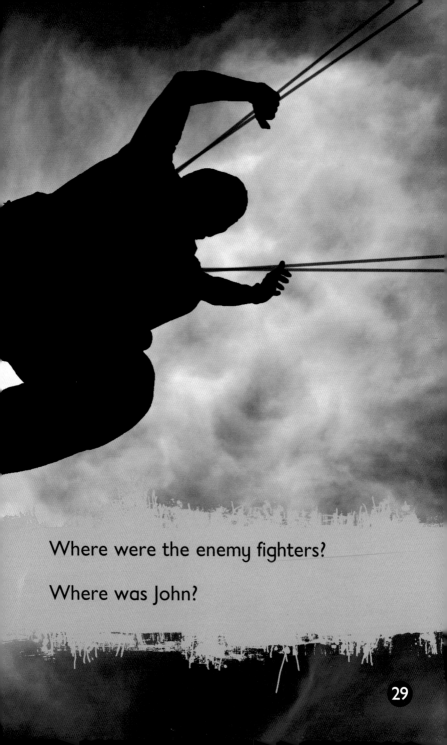

Where were the enemy fighters?

Where was John?

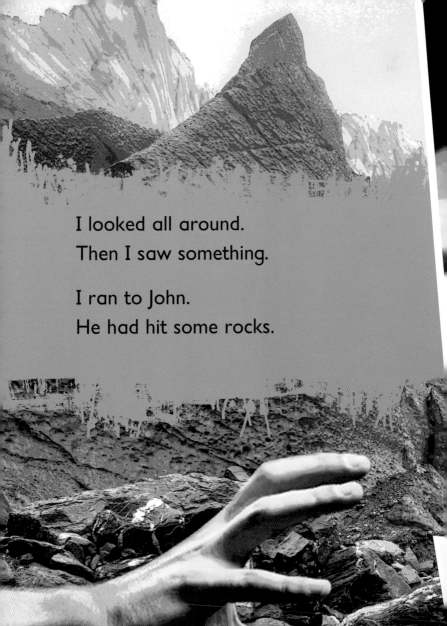

I looked all around.
Then I saw something.

I ran to John.
He had hit some rocks.

He said, "Help me, Mark."
I said, "You'll be OK, Mate."

His legs were broken.
His head was bleeding.

31

I got on the radio
to the base.

I said, "We're in
trouble. How soon
can you get here?"

There was
a problem.
A big problem.

A huge storm was heading straight for us.

The rescue helicopters could not fly in the storm.

There was another problem.
I could see the enemy fighters.
They were about a kilometre away.

We had to hide.

If they found us — they would kill us.

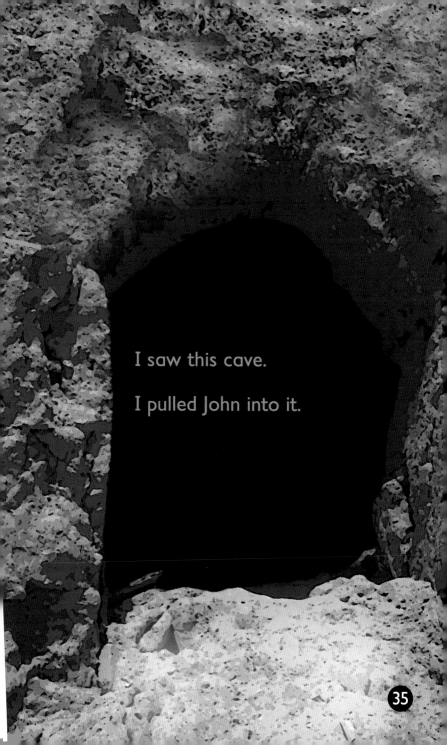

I saw this cave.

I pulled John into it.

Inside the cave we waited.
Outside we could hear shouting.

The shouting got nearer
and nearer.

John was moaning.

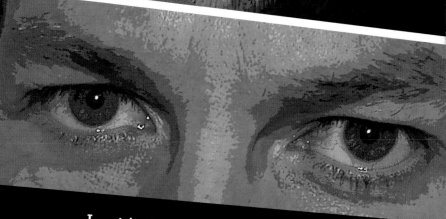

I said, "Keep quiet, Mate."

Then the storm hit.

It's morning.
It is light outside.
Suddenly we hear voices.

The voices get nearer
and nearer.

We wait.

It's our guys!

A soldier says, "It's good to see you guys."
He says, "We're taking you both home!"

Our helicopters land outside.

John is in a lot of pain.
But we are going to be OK.

I say, "We're going to be
OK, Mate."

"I'll buy you that
beer, soon."

EJECT, EJECT, **EJECT - WHAT'S NEXT?**

TORNADOES
ON YOUR OWN

The fighter jet in this book is a Tornado. Find out more facts about this plane online.

Draw a diagram or use a photograph of a tornado to create a fact file about the plane.

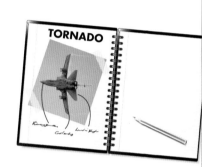

HAVING A BEER
WITH A PARTNER

Imagine that the pilots Mark and John meet up in the bar back at the base. It's a few weeks after the crash and John is in a wheelchair. Mark buys John that beer he promised him!

- Discuss how each character would feel.
- Discuss what they would talk about.
- Role-play the conversation that the two characters have.

SURVIVORS
IN A GROUP

Your plane has crashed in the mountains. A storm is coming in. You need to find shelter. You don't know when you will be rescued.

- As a group, choose the ten most useful items from the plane that will help you survive.
- Rank your items in order of importance.
- Time yourselves – can you make a decision in under half an hour?

FIGHTER PILOT
ON YOUR OWN / WITH A PARTNER / IN A GROUP

Mark's job is to attack enemy aircraft in the air or to bomb enemies on the ground. It took him four years to train as a fighter pilot.

HAVE YOU GOT
WHAT IT TAKES?

- What kind of person would make a good fighter pilot? Make a list of words to describe them.
- Look online. What skills do fighter pilots need to learn? Make a list of these.
- Make a poster advertising a course for trainee fighter pilots.
- Role-play an interview for a trainee fighter pilot.

IF YOU ENJOYED
THIS BOOK,
TRY THESE OTHER
RiGHT NOW!
BOOKS.

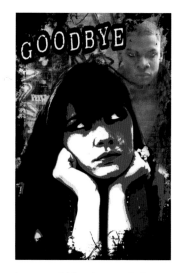

Lucy and Lloyd were in love,
but now it's over. So why is
Lloyd always watching her?

Alisha's online messages to
new girl Sam get nastier and
nastier. Will anyone help Sam?

Steve hates what he sees in
the mirror. Lizzie does, too.
Their lives would be so much
better if they looked different.

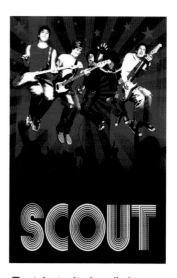

It's Saturday night.
Two angry guys. Two knives.
There's going to be a fight.

Tonight is the band's big
chance. Tonight, a record
company scout is at their gig!

Ed's platoon is under attack.
Another soldier is in danger.
Ed must risk his own life to
save him.

It's just an old, empty house.
Lauren must spend the night
inside. Just Lauren and
the ghost...

Dan sees the red car.
The keys are inside. Dan says
to Andy, Sam and Jess,
"Want to go for a drive?"

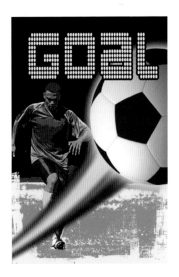

Today is Carl's trial with
City. There's just one place
up for grabs. But today,
everything is going wrong!

Sophie hates this new town.
She misses her friends.
There's nowhere to skate!

Tonight, Vicky must make a
choice. Stay in London with
her boyfriend Chris. Or start
a new life in Australia.